ALAN EDWARDS was born in England and was brought up and educated in Kenya. He returned to England to take his accountancy examinations and became a qualified accountant. He has spent his working life in accountancy and has worked in Kenya, the old Belgian Congo and Belgium and is now retired.

The Land of Puff

The Land of Puff

Alan Edwards

ATHENA PRESS
LONDON

The Land of Puff
Copyright © Alan Edwards 2009

ISBN: 978 1 84748 455 0

First published 2009 by
ATHENA PRESS
Queen's House, 2 Holly Road
Twickenham TW1 4EG
United Kingdom

Printed for Athena Press

Illustrations are by the author

TWO   PUFF

THEY MUST ALL HOP

They Must All Hop

Puff, the puffin, was watching his feet as he walked along the uneven path, but his tummy kept getting in the way. Trouble was that, in trying to see round his bulge, he stumbled, as he could not watch out for the stones in his path at the same time.

He came to a halt, swaying slightly, when he heard a voice say, 'Puff, what are you doing?'

Puff looked up and said, 'Oh, it's you, Two. Go away, you are no help.' His head dropped onto his chest as he contemplated for a while. Nothing happened and, changing from one foot to the same foot, Two asked, 'Are you sure I can be of no help?'

Puff looked up and tried to see which foot Two, the dodo, was standing on. This made him go cross-eyed. Puff cocked his head on one side and thought for a moment or two. *After all*, he thought, *it could not do any harm to ask him. There was no one else about. I could always pretend it had not happened.* He often pretended things hadn't happened.

'I read the other day,' began Puff, 'that most people wear out their right foot faster than their left. I was trying to find out why. I am sure there must be a reason. People will think I am clever if I discover the reason. I was trying to see if I could tell which one was wearing out faster than the other, but have become tired of walking and trying to look at my feet at the same time. They were made for swimming in the sea, not stumbling on these stones in the path. Furthermore, neither of them looks worn out yet.'

As he finished saying this, he tried to pick up his left foot to peer at it. He was not built for such gymnastics. He nearly fell over. This made him put his foot down hard on a sharp stone, which hurt him. He sat down and rubbed it slowly.

'I have the advantage over you, Puff,' said Two. 'Both of mine are left feet. Whichever wears out first cannot be wrong, and will not be my right foot. Why don't you hop?'

'Hop what?' asked Puff.

'I mean hop on your left foot,' said Two. 'Then it would have to wear out first.' He looked smug as he said this. He thought he had been clever again. He was always thinking that.

Puff climbed slowly to his feet. He gave one or two hops and then a few more. His eyes lit up and his feathers fell about. His bulge in the middle wobbled like an unset jelly. He came to a halt, puffing a little.

'A most excellent suggestion, Two,' he said. He started to hop down the path, shouting as he went. 'I will pass a law, pass a law. They will all have to hop. Then we will see who is right, no I mean left. No matter, it will be law, will be law, will be law…' Then, he vanished out of sight.

Two went on down the path, still looking smug. He had to keep to a path if he wanted to walk straight. Out in the open he walked round in a circle to the left. This was sad to see, as he usually fell over in the end.

Turning a bend in the path, he came upon Far, the guillemot. Far was always far from the shore, and that's how he got his name. He was sitting all alone on a rock, looking at the sky in a dreamy sort of way. He looked at Two and, brushing his feathers from his eyes, said, 'Puff has just passed by and he was hopping on one foot, most strange. Do you know why, Two?'

'Yes, Far, I do,' replied Two, drawing himself up. He now had an audience so he could speak. 'He was not just hopping on one foot, he was hopping on his left foot. I trust you will take note of this most important correction. Now, as for your question, you will have noticed that I have two left feet. Puff wants us to wear out our left foot first. This will prove what I have always maintained: that there is no right, only left, and I have both of them.' He paused, for he had lost his train of thought as usual. 'What did you ask me, Far?'

'Why was Puff hopping on his left foot?' repeated Far, getting it right this time.

'Oh yes,' said Two remembering. 'He is going to pass a law making us all hop on our left foot. This will ensure that we wear out our left foot first. We will then be able to prove that it does more work than the right.'

'Very logical,' replied Far. 'I must practise at once.' He tucked his right foot under one wing and made a few hops with his left. He was not very good at it, but then, he was not very good at anything much.

He stopped and looked at Two. He realised that Two would not have to hop as he had two left feet. Even if they wore out half as slowly, they were still both left feet. He did not say anything. He would have to think of a way of getting his own back on Two. The smug look on Two's face did not help.

'Let us go and find Puff,' said Two, starting to walk on again.

'Good idea, Two,' said Far, hopping behind him. 'After you,' he said with a smile.

Two walked on. Two could not see behind himself without stopping and turning round. Far was then able to stop hopping and walk on both feet. This was much more comfortable for him. *I will practise again tomorrow*, he thought to himself.

He ambled along behind Two, putting as much weight as possible on his left foot. This made him a bit one-sided. *I must always do as Puff tells me, even if I am not sure why*, he mused. But he could not help wondering what would happen when their left feet wore out. 'Never mind, Puff will know,' he reassured himself, and they continued on down the road to the House of Hot Air.

Shell Out the Shells

Two and Far arrived at the House of Hot Air to find that most of the penguins were assembled. They were milling about looking lost, waiting to be told what to do. On seeing Two and Far, some of them rushed forward shouting:

'Where is Puff?'

'When will we be told what to do?'

'Why have we all been called here today?'

Two and Far did not bother to reply, but pushed past them and went straight to the Inner Sanctum. As they walked through, Far was relieved to see that none of the penguins were hopping. *So, Puff has not yet made it law*, he thought to himself. *Let's hope he forgets.*

Puff was at the table in the sanctum with Doc Owl. As they came in, he said, 'But I do not understand, why are there too many shells?'

'Because Doc forgot to count them,' said a voice from the corner. It was Jack, the woodpecker, sitting quietly by himself.

'That is not true,' shouted Doc. 'I told them to keep a count themselves as I was too busy to do it.'

'Who is "them"?' asked Puff.

'The people who give out the shells from the Mint Hole,' said Jack. 'They were supposed to count them as they gave them out. They were told to write the numbers down. They knew Doc was too busy to check what they did. So they gave out more shells, without writing them down, when people like Two wanted them.

'Is that true, Two?' asked Puff. 'Did you take shells from the Mint Hole without permission, and not write them down?'

'I gave myself permission,' replied Two. 'I am just as important as Doc, and if he can order more shells, then so can I. If I want more shells I will take them.'

'That is all very well,' replied Doc. 'I get all the blame when things go wrong and the penguins outside shout at me. They say nasty things to me when it is not my fault. You just sit back and look smug. There are now too many shells in everyone's pocket, all because you took too many out of the Mint Hole.' He sniffed and looked as if he was about to cry.

Puff patted him on the head and said, 'Now, now, Doc, do not get upset, Puff will find a way out of this problem. I will ask Jack. He is good at solving problems.' Puff did not know how to solve the problem himself, but he was not going to tell them that. Puff turned to Jack and said, 'Let us hear your solution to this problem.'

'There is a simple solution,' said Jack. 'Thanks to Two, there are now too many shells in our pockets. If we pass a law, making everything twice as expensive, we have solved the problem.'

Puff looked puzzled. 'I do not see how that can be a solution,' he said, in the hope that no one else understood either. He did not wish to look like a fool.

'Well,' replied Jack, 'suppose you have four shells in your pocket and you need two for your fish for supper. We make a law making everything twice as expensive. The fish will now cost you four shells. You pay over your four shells. You now have a nice fish for your supper.'

SHELL OUT THE SHELLS

Puff began to think about his supper and said quickly, 'That all sounds very sensible. Good, we will make a new law. Has anyone any questions?'

Far was puzzled and said, in a dazed sort of way, 'But then Puff will have used up all his shells and will have none left.'

'That is right,' replied Jack. 'When his fish cost two shells, he did not need the other two. So it is the same really. If Puff needs any more, we can always take some more from the Mint Hole for him.'

'That is good,' replied Far. 'I did not want Puff to go without his supper.'

They all started to pack up their papers. They wanted to go out to tell the penguins, when suddenly Doc said, 'Wait a moment. It all sounds very easy, but how does it solve my problem?'

Jack replied. 'You first make everything twice as expensive. That is the same as making the shells only half what they were before. In that way you have not issued too many shells. Then, as you know, we take away half of the penguins' shells as a tax to pay us for looking after them so well. You may have issued too many shells, but now you will be able to collect twice as much, which means you will then have more to spend on us.'

When he heard this, Doc looked pleased and rubbed his wings in glee. He liked the thought of having more shells to spend. He had not realised that the shells he would now be collecting would only be worth half as much. *You* can see that, but Puff and Doc did not.

They then trooped out of the sanctum together. They were greeted by the cheers of the penguins who were waiting to be told what to do.

The King's Army

P uff did not like armies very much. However, he did like some soldiers. He would prefer some, with feathers in their hats, standing guard outside his house. They would escort him when he went out and that would make everyone look at him. He would like that. All he had were just a few toy soldiers and they were a tatty lot. None of them had feathers in their hats and some of them where chipped and broken.

He was setting out his toy soldiers on the ground one day. He was thinking how important he would look if he could ride at their head, sitting on a white horse, when a voice cried, 'Halt in the name of the king.'

Puff jumped; he had not heard anyone coming and it had given him a fright. He recognised the voice. It was Titch the Kingfisher. He was a bit frightened of him and, to cover this, he always talked in a loud voice to him and was sometimes very rude.

'What do you want, Titch, creeping up on me like that? Why did you cry out in the name of the king?'

'Because that is the king's army you are playing with, or rather, what is left of it is his. I see you have broken some more soldiers. You will not have any left soon. Then what will you play with?' replied Titch.

Puff ignored the last question, as he did not know the

PUFF   CARVER   TWO

THE KING'S ARMY

answer. Perhaps if he said nothing Titch would forget he had asked it. Instead, Puff replied, 'It is not the king's army any more. It belongs to me now.'

'The soldiers wear the king's uniform. They swear to serve king and country when they join, so how is it yours now?' asked Titch.

Puff looked sly and replied, 'It is still called the king's army, but he has no power over them. I am now the one who points and tells them who and where the enemy is.'

'Don't they mind?' asked Titch.

'Of course not,' replied Puff, in an important sort of way. 'The King stopped riding at the head of his army a long time ago. His army was taken away from him and given to the people to protect themselves from him.'

'Sounds daft,' replied Titch. 'Anyway, *you* are not "the people", so how did you get them?'

'Ah, but I *am* the people,' replied Puff. 'They made me their leader and I have taken over the army on their behalf. So now I can do as I please with them.' Mind you, Puff had no intention of riding at their head into battle; he might get hurt. As he finished speaking, he turned and kicked one of the soldiers.

'Stop that,' said Titch sharply. 'There is no need to take your bad temper out on them. Whatever you say, it is still the king's army. You should look after it carefully. After all, you might need them to protect you one day.'

Puff did not reply, and Titch could see he had lost interest in talking to him. Titch wanted to talk to his friends about the king's army, or was it the people's army? It did all seem a bit odd, so he hurried off to find them.

He left just in time, for who should come round the corner to see Puff but Two, followed by Carver the turkey. Two interrupted Puff's thoughts by saying very loudly, 'I am glad to see you have put out all your soldiers, Puff. We can now get rid of them once and for all. You are too old to play with soldiers, and they give you bad ideas.'

Puff would normally have let him ramble on, as he had heard it all before. His soldiers did not give him much fun now that Doc had stopped them from making loud bangs. Doc said it cost too much. He noticed that Carver, who was standing behind Doc, was snivelling. 'What are you weeping about, Carver?' he asked.

'If Two makes you throw away your soldiers,' sniffed Carver, 'I will not have anything to do. I will become like a penguin. No one will salute me. No one will drive me about in a big car with a flag on it. I will not even be taken up in an aeroplane or...' He did not finish, but pulled out a handkerchief and blew his nose loudly. He was a very sad sight.

Puff then remembered that he had made Carver the head of the army. *Silly thing to have done*, he mused, *but I felt sorry for him. I can also make him take the blame if anything goes wrong. That could be very useful.* Then, turning to Two, he said, 'Tell you what, Two, we will take these soldiers over here, remove their guns, which do not work anyway, and put them in this shed. Now they are not real soldiers any more, just scribes. Does that make you happy? We will call them "The Two-foot Pen Pushers" and you can be their unpaid colonel. How about that?'

Two felt very proud at having some soldiers named after him, and he shuffled off happily to tell his friend Far about it. Carver did not mind what they were called, or what they did, just so long as he still had an army to be head of. He was not sure how Puff had been able to satisfy Two so easily, but that was not his worry.

Puff was deep in thought as he walked back to the House of Hot Air. He realised that Two liked to feel important, and this gave him an idea. If he, Puff, could become a droll, then Two would have to take over as leader. ('Droll' is the prefix given to anyone who is a member of the upper house.) Puff would not have to worry about all the problems any more. He could hear the words in his thoughts, *Arise, Droll Puff-Puff.* That thought cheered him up and he walked on briskly, chirping as he went.

THE NEW BEAT

The New Boat

Carver frowned as he hurried along. He had been called to the Inner Sanctum by Puff. He could not think why. Carver did not think he had done anything wrong, but you could never tell with Puff. Carver had been away for some days and did not know what had changed from not wrong to wrong while he was away. *Ah well*, he thought, *there is nothing for it, I will have to just go in and find out.*

Carver went in to the Inner Sanctum and took his place at the table. He noticed that all the others were already there and that Puff was looking very pleased with himself. There was a large box-shaped thing on the table in front of Puff, covered by a cloth.

Puff called the meeting to order by saying, 'Now that Carver is here we can start our business. I have called you all together as we are having a bit of a problem with our navy. I think we have found the answer. I wanted to hear your views on it.'

Oh, dear, thought Jack, *that means he thinks he has been clever again and wants us all to say yes to something.*

Puff went on, 'As you know, all the old navy boats were full of guns and bullets and engines and things. There was very little room for the crew. They had to sleep in hammocks in the same place that they worked and ate their food. It was most uncomfortable for them, though they did not seem to mind. We do not think this is right or... do I mean it is wrong? No matter. We have therefore decided to change things.'

He paused for breath and looked about. Most of the others had nodded off with their heads under their wings. This made him cross – all his lovely words falling on deaf ears. He banged hard on the table and they all woke up with a start. 'If you do not pay attention I will send you out to join the penguins, instead of sitting in the warm with me.' These words had the desired effect and they all sat up and looked alert. Puff went on, 'We have to build a new boat, as our old one is worn out and leaks. It cannot put to sea any more, which is a pity.'

'Does that matter?' asked Two. 'And what do we need a new one for anyway?'

'I need one, or rather *we* do,' replied Puff. 'We will use it for giving rides to important people. We will visit other lands to show how important we are. The other lands have lots of them and they sail everywhere. Everybody thinks they are much more important than us when they only see their boats.'

Just as well, thought Jack. *Our captain does not get much practice. When he does go out to sea, he has a habit of bumping into things.*

Puff went on. 'I therefore asked the men who make boats to send me a model. This is for a new boat, designed by me, and here it is.' With that, he removed the cloth from the box-like thing on the table. Far started to clap, but the others glared at him and Doc kicked him under the table, so he stopped. He did, however, notice that Puff looked pleased with him. He was glad he had clapped, even if the others did not like it.

Puff gazed in admiration at the model, which looked a bit odd really. The hull was made of wood and shaped like a bathtub. The top part was square, with lots of windows. There was a mast on top with a flag, which was a little bent. Puff straightened it out. The flag had a puffin head on it. There were paddle wheels on each side, and a large rudder at the back.

'Let me explain,' said Puff. 'You all know how safe bathtubs are. They hold lots of water and never leak, unless, of course, you pull the plug out. They do not tip up when you sit in them. So, the new boat is shaped like a bathtub. It is made of wood so it will float better. Is that all clear to you?'

Jack was about to say that bathtubs, as a rule, had water inside and were not put on water to float. He decided to keep quiet for a while. Puff went on. 'The top is designed to give each man his own room with a window. There is a football pitch in the middle. There are also lots more interesting things inside. I have a list somewhere, if I can find it, which tells you what they all are.'

'Why paddle wheels?' asked Jack.

'Well, that was another idea of mine,' replied Puff. 'The right one goes forward and the left one backwards, or is it the other way round? It is of no matter.'

'Would that not make it go round in a circle?' asked Jack.

'Well, yes and no,' replied Puff. 'That is why we have such a large rudder. It starts to go round in a circle, but the rudder stops it and it goes along sideways like a crab. Mind you it can only turn one way, which is a bit inconvenient.'

'I am glad you have not put any guns on the boat,' said Doc. 'They are expensive to buy and the sailors always want to play with them. It costs me a lot of money every time they fire one off. They also make a loud noise, and have a nasty smell as well.'

'May I see it float?' asked Carver, as he liked to play with boats in his bath.

'Certainly not,' retorted Puff. 'It might get wet.'

No one seemed to know what to say after that. Boats are supposed to get wet, well on the outside at least. *I wonder if it does float*, thought Jack. *It must do, Puff would have tested it. Would he have dared not to have tested it?* Jack was not sure.

The meeting then came to an end, and the cover was put back on the boat. They were left wondering what they had all agreed to and why. Puff knew, as he had already written it all down. They took comfort in the thought that none of them had suggested the new boat. They could not be blamed if it all went wrong, didn't even float, and wouldn't go straight. Puff had other thoughts. If he could get his drollship before the boat was built, Two would be in charge. Two would get the blame if it did not float. *Serve him right*, thought Puff and, feeling much more cheerful, he joined the others outside.

Buried Treasure

Puff was upset. He walked up and down in an agitated sort of way. He sat down, stood up and started walking up and down again. Jack watched him out of the corner of his eye, but said nothing. Far was worried because Puff was worried, though he did not know why. Nobody said anything. They were all too busy thinking up excuses in case Puff tried to blame them for whatever it was that was wrong. Doc tried to slip out, but Puff had seen him and made him sit down again. The others sniggered, as this made him look a fool. They did not always like Doc, for he had a habit of lecturing them. He was very pompous at times.

The problem was caused by a hole that was being dug to find some treasure. A very important person had said it was in a field. Puff did not know where it was in the field. This made it rather difficult to find. Puff needed the treasure. He was running short of shells to buy things. He did not want to take any more from the Mint Hole as that did not work. The price of everything then went up and up. Even worse, Doc had a habit of saying 'I told you so', which made him very irritable.

They first had to find a way of locating the treasure without digging up all the field. This was not easy, as it was a rather big field. They had all been standing about making suggestions when Two had walked onto the field. He started to shuffle round in a circle, fell over his feet, and got his beak stuck in the ground. 'This is the spot,' he had shouted, as he was helped to his feet by Far. 'It must be here or I would not have fallen over.'

Puff did not agree, but he did not know how to pick another spot that was any better. He had to accept Two's beak mark. Titch had been watching all this, sitting on a fence post. He was rather enjoying making suggestions and comments. He felt quite safe because it was not his problem. He could therefore say what he liked to embarrass Puff.

'That looks like a silly way to pick a place to dig,' he shouted. 'However, if you are determined to dig a hole there, make sure it is square. They are easier to dig than round ones,' he added.

He should not have said that, because Two replied immediately, 'My hole will be a round one.' That was how a round hole was decided upon. But it did not get dug very quickly. It took days to agree the size of the circle, with a lot of shouting and bad tempers. In the end, Puff had to draw the circle himself so that work could start.

The reason for Puff's present worry was the cost of digging the hole. There were all the people just standing about who had to be paid, and they had not found any treasure yet. Puff spoke at last and, turning to Doc, asked, 'How many shells have I paid to the diggers so far?'

Doc had been busy doing sums on pieces of paper and was in a state of confusion. This was not surprising, for he had bits of paper everywhere. Some had fallen on the floor and some had been hidden by Jack under a large shell. 'I keep coming up with a different answer. So far, all I know is that it comes to lots and lots. But do not worry; I have borrowed some shells from our friends over the water, to pay for the diggers. They will know how many shells I have

BURIED TREASURE

borrowed. They are better at adding up than I am. They know I will pay them back when we find the treasure,' he replied.

'If we find the treasure,' muttered Jack, to himself.

At this point Two spoke up. 'You are not paying anybody any shells. You are borrowing some shells from our friends to give to the diggers. You will then pay our friends back with the treasure you find. That way the digging does not cost you anything. You can easily borrow some more, can't he, Puff?' he said, turning to Puff and catching him unawares.

Puff was not sure. He did not think it right to borrow more shells. He did not have a better solution, so he replied, 'Yes, of course, Doc can borrow more, for we must keep digging. We need the treasure.'

He had been thinking. He realised that he would probably receive his drollship just before the field was all dug up. Two would be left to face their unhappy friends from over the water, without any treasure to repay them. If, on the other hand, the treasure was found before his droll day, then he would have all the credit for being so clever. He began to feel smug. 'You go ahead and borrow all you need, Doc,' he added.

Far then spoke for the first time. 'What happens if we do not find the treasure, and are not able to pay our friends back?' he asked, with a puzzled frown.

Puff had hoped that no one would ask this question. He could not tell them his thoughts. He did not have to, as Two immediately broke in and said, 'Of course we will find the treasure. We are always right. We will have to borrow some more shells if it takes a little longer. Is that not so, Puff?' Puff just nodded his agreement. Two had fallen into the trap. He did not know how he had done so.

Far brooded over all this with his head on his chest, and then looked up to speak again, but it was too late. They had all left and the room was empty and silent. *Ah well*, he thought, *Puff knows best. He will find a way of finding the shells so that it will all come out right in the end, even if the cost of digging for the treasure is more than the value of the treasure itself. At least I will not be blamed for it. I have had nothing to do with it.* With that comforting thought he left the room and went home quietly.

BRITANICUS

TWO   PUFF   DOC   JACK

THE BALLOON MAKERS

The Balloon Makers

Puff did not like problems being brought to him to solve, because it meant he had to take a side and the loser would be unhappy. Puff would then have to give the loser something to make him happy. He had no way of knowing which were the pretend problems and which were the real ones. He had just been caught out by Two, as he had not been on his guard. The conversation had started on the balcony of the House of Hot Air.

'Puff, did you know that another balloon factory closed today? All the people who worked in it now have no work,' said Two.

'Now that is not quite true,' replied Puff. 'We have told them that they will be paid exactly the same. They do not have to work. The only problem with doing this is that it costs so much. It was not too bad when they still made some balloons. We did receive some shells back as a tribute from them. Now more goes out than comes back. Doc is very unhappy about it all as well,' ended Puff in a mournful sort of way. He looked very sad with all his feathers drooping over his face.

'True, true,' replied Two softly. 'Pity we cannot put my scheme into operation. Then we would not have to pay out all those shells. But still, I am sure you have more important things to think about. You do not want to be bothered by my silly scheme. Sad, really, when you think about all the shells you could save and then spend on other things.'

Puff perked up immediately. His feathers stood up again, when he heard this. 'Do you have a scheme that will save money by not paying the out-of-work balloon makers?' he asked.

'Yes,' replied Two, in a very humble sort of way as he shuffled his two left feet. 'I could tell you all about it at our Friday meeting if you like. Then, if no one likes it, no harm will have been done. If they like it, that will be fine because we will have lots of spare shells to spend.'

'Good,' replied Puff. 'I will see you on Friday.' Then, deep in thought, but with a skip or two, he went off thinking of shells and the things he could spend them on.

Friday came and they were all assembled in the Inner Sanctum. Puff called the meeting to order and said, 'I have asked Two to present a proposal to you, which I am sure you will like. Carry on, Two.'

Two lumbered onto his feet, looking very important. 'The proposal is a suggested way we could save lots of shells. We will not be paying the out-of-work balloon makers for doing no work.' This made them all sit up and take notice. Saving money to spend was something very dear to their hearts.

Two unrolled a map of Britanicus. He had marked each balloon factory that had closed with a red dot. Around each red dot he had drawn a green circle. The map looked very pretty. Two cleared his throat, took a sip of water, and continued. 'My idea is quite simple. The inside of each green circle will be called Loon Land. In Loon Land, the only people who will be able to work will be the out-of-work balloon makers. We will then not have to go on paying them for not working.' He then sat down looking smug.

There was a stunned silence. Puff realised he had been caught and did not know what to do. He said, thinking quickly, 'I will ask each of you for your comments before we take a vote on Two's proposal.' He was hoping they would all say 'no'. Then he would not have to decide anything. He turned to Doc. 'Well, Doc, what do you think about it?'

'In general, I am in agreement, but I will have to study it in more detail before I could agree to it,' replied Doc, a little worried, as he did not like saying yes.

Puff looked at Far, and raised his eyebrows, inviting comment.

'Well, in so much as the scheme has been put forward by Two, I will support it. I will not try to understand what it is all about. It is far too complicated,' replied Far, brushing the feathers back from his eyes.

Puff began to get worried. He was not doing very well. He turned to Jack and asked, 'Have you any comments?'

'You must be in Loon Land already if you are prepared to agree to the rubbish Two has just presented. Why not teach them to make something else? They could then find other work and we could stop paying them for not working.' Jack was very cross and would have continued, but Doc butted in.

'We cannot afford to teach them to make something else,' he said. 'If we do that, I will not have the money we save to spend.'

'Doc,' said Puff very quickly, 'Let me make one thing clear, if any money is saved, I will spend it, not you.'

'Oh,' replied Doc very peeved. 'If that is the case, I am sorry I said I agreed with the scheme.'

'Wait a moment,' shouted Two. 'It is my scheme, so I should be the one who has the saved shells to spend.'

'Stop this bickering, all of you,' said Puff in a stern voice. He continued when quiet was established. 'If you will agree to the scheme, we will all share the savings. Each person will write down, on a piece of paper, what they want to spend the saved shells on. The papers will then be put in my hat. Later, I will draw out three of them. They will be the ones we spend the saved shells on.'

There was silence for a moment, and then they all agreed, except Jack. He was still shouting. 'You are all mad loonies... mad... mad!' he screamed, to an empty room. The others had all rushed off to find a piece of paper. They wrote down their pet scheme on their piece of paper. Then they returned to put their pieces of paper in Puff's hat.

Puff was very relieved. He had control over his own hat. 'I will secretly mark them. Then I will only draw out the ones I want,' he said to himself. *But it was a very near thing and I was nearly caught out by Two. I must be more careful in future*, he thought, as he pulled his best feathered hat from the cupboard. He brushed off the dust and placed it on the table, ready for the pieces of paper to be placed in it.

The Up and Down Muddle

Puff was very angry. His mouth opened and closed, but no sound came out. The cause of his anger, Titch, was sitting opposite him in the great hall. He seemed to enjoy Puff making a fool of himself. Taking a deep breath, Puff at last found his voice. 'No!' he shouted. 'A thousand times: no! I will not agree to your proposal. Never, never, never.'

All this bother had started the day before. The House of Hot Air was full of penguins at the time. The bell rang, calling them all to their places. Some were upstairs and had to come down. Some were downstairs and had to go up. When they heard the bell they all rushed to find their places.

They bumped into each other and were all mixed up. Two tried to go down the stairs. He fell over his feet and rolled down the stairs to the bottom. He knocked over all the penguins trying to come up the stairs. They all ended up at the bottom in a pile of arms, legs and bent feathers. No one was injured, but some had bumps and bruises, which hurt them.

The next day, Titch stood up in the great hall and said, 'My friendly and not-so-friendly penguins, I have a proposal to make. I suggest that, as from today, everybody using the stairs walks on the right side. That way, no one will bump into anyone else. There will not be any more nasty accidents like the one we saw yesterday.' He sat down with a smile. There was absolute silence for a moment, then everyone began to shout. The umpire banged on the table and the noise died down. It was then that everybody saw how angry Puff was.

When Puff had finished, Two stood up and said, 'There is only one way to go up and down stairs. It is the left side – the side I always use. I, therefore, make a counter proposal. As from today, everyone using the stairs must walk on the left side.' He sat down, and all the penguins behind him cheered and stamped their feet.

Titch was first to speak, after the noise died down. 'May I suggest we stop for lunch now. Puff and I will eat our fish together and talk this over. We will meet again in an hour.' He then walked out with Puff to find a quiet place to talk.

Two tried to follow them, shouting, 'Down the left! I mean, up the left.' In his hurry to follow them he fell over his feet. He struggled to his feet, but he was too late. Both Puff and Titch had vanished. Muttering to himself, he shuffled off to find his food.

Puff and Titch found a quiet place under a tree. They opened their packets of fish and started to eat. After a while, Puff spoke. 'My dear Titch, you have a problem.'

'No I do not,' he replied. 'It is you who has the problem, not I. Your problem is Two, and his two left feet.'

'Come, come,' replied Puff. 'Even if you make the right side the law, Two will have to use the left side. He has to walk on the left side. Then what would you do? Lock him up? You know that you cannot do that. Two is above the law when he is in the House of Hot Air. So, the left side it will have to be.'

Titch thought for a while. He could not let Puff win so easily. At last he spoke. 'The stairs are too wide anyway. We will divide them in two. We will build a wall in the middle.

THE UP DOWN MUDDLE

'We will call one side left and the other right. Then, if you use the left one, you go up and down on the left side. If you use the right one, you go up and down on the right. That way, everybody will be happy. We will not have to make any new laws.'

Puff considered this for a moment. He could not tell Titch that he could not tell his left from his right. This could put him in a muddle if he agreed. 'Well, yes,' he replied. 'I can agree to your suggestion, but will need a change made to your plan. Each side must be clearly marked with the words 'left' and 'right'. There will also be a big arrow showing the way to go.' This way, Puff would not get in a muddle. He would only have to follow the signs.

'I think I can agree to that,' replied Titch. They brushed the crumbs from their feathers and stood up. Titch continued, 'Let us go and tell the others what we have agreed.' They both returned to the House of Hot Air. They were then both able to tell their own penguins how each had been able to persuade the other, and that it was their suggestion that had been agreed. So ended the up and down muddle.

The Other Side of the Road

Puff walked out of the House of Hot Air one spring morning. He ambled across the pavement and stepped straight out into the road without looking. There was a shout and a squeal of breaks. A taxi came to a halt just in time, only inches from Puff. The driver leaned out and shouted, 'Why do you not look where you are going?'

Puff looked up with a start. He realised just how close he had come to being run over. He was cross and shouted back, 'No one shouts at me. I walk where I want to.' He waved his wings about and flapped his feet on the ground saying, 'Do you know who I am? I am Puff and you do not shout at me! Drive round me and go away.'

Puff stood for a moment in the middle of the road. The people driving on the road had to go round him. He then waddled back to the pavement and returned to his sanctum. He rang his bell to call his friends together. They all stopped what they were doing when they heard the bell and rushed to the sanctum.

They all sat at the table looking apprehensive. They did not like being called so suddenly. Puff tapped on the table and addressed them. 'I was nearly run over by a taxi just now, right outside the House of Hot Air. This must not happen again. I will make a law to stop people running into me. They will all have to use the other side of the road. Then they will have plenty of time to see me and stop. I shall make a law and that will be that.' He paused for a moment and looked round the table. No one said anything. They were far to busy trying to understand what Puff had said. It was not easy for them to think.

Two was the first to break the silence. 'No, I cannot agree to that. If everybody goes over to the other side, they will no longer be on the left side, where they are supposed to be.'

'That is not so,' replied Far. 'They would still be on the left side, but on the other side. I mean—' He did not finish. Jack had kicked him under the table. The kick hurt and made him forget what he was going to say.

'I have to disagree with you, Puff,' said Doc. 'If they have to drive on the other side, all the road signs would have to be changed. That would cost a lot of money.'

Puff began to feel cross. He did not like it when people did not agree with him. He could not think of a reply. Doc and Two were right and not wrong. He began to think he would have to agree with them. Then, Carver spoke up for the first time.

'Well, as you know,' he began in a humble sort of way, 'I have, or rather, *we* have some soldiers who sit on horses all day. They look very smart, they do, with long feathers in their hats and big, polished, black boots. Some of them have nowhere to sit on their horses all day. This is a pity, as people like to see them sitting outside important places. I thought we could have four of them outside the House of Hot Air. Then Puff could cross the road in safety. When they see Puff coming, they could ride their horses out into the road and stop all the traffic. Puff could then cross the road in peace. No one would bump into him.' He stopped quite exhausted, for he seldom said so many words at one time.

THE OTHER SIDE OF THE ROAD

Puff was delighted with this. 'Thank you, Carver. That is a very good idea.' He liked it all the better because Two would be upset. Two was always trying to get rid of Puff's soldiers. He could not get rid of the soldiers if they were doing important work. Doc would be put out as well. He was always complaining about the cost of the hay the horses ate, as well as the polish for the boots. *Serves them both right for not agreeing with me*, thought Puff.

They then had no choice but to all agree with Carver's suggestion. Doc had to pay for the four boxes the horses stood in. Two was upset because there were always lots of people looking at them. He could not get rid of them now. Carver went out every day, when Puff was not looking, to inspect them. They saluted him with their swords. This made him feel very important, especially if there were lots of people about.

Puff loved it. He found many excuses for going out of the House of Hot Air. He took great pleasure in seeing the horses ride out into the road, with the soldiers sitting on them, waving their swords about. The cars stopped on either side as he ambled over the road. The people watching cheered. The soldiers on the horses then placed their swords in front of themselves to salute him. *Now everybody knows who I am and that is how it should be*, he said to himself, as he proudly pattered between them for the tenth time that day.

The Left-winged Door

Two was right-winged. This was odd considering he had two left feet. You would have thought he would have been left-winged. This caused Two a problem. Each time he went towards a door, his feet would take him to the left. His right wing would then miss the handle. More often than not, he would bump into the door post, which was a painful experience for him.

Two tried to make himself left-winged, thinking this might help. He tried to write with his left wing, but then no one could read his writing. He even tried to open doors with his left wing, but had little success.

Two was practising one day in front of a door and was seen by Far. Far stood and watched Two but did not say anything. Two was not doing very well and, after he had bumped into the door post for the third time, Far spoke up and said, 'Why do you keep bumping into the door post, Two?'

Two was startled and jumped a little. He had not known that Far was watching him. This made him fall over his feet, and he bumped the door post for the fourth time. He rubbed his head and, in a very grumpy voice, said, 'Now look what you have made me do. Why are you creeping about, giving me a fright?' He went on rubbing his head and sat down on a bench. Far stood his ground and waited.

TWO

THE LEFT WINGED DOOR

Realising that Far would not go away, Two said, 'I was trying to open that door with my left wing.'

'Why do you want to do that?' asked Far, for he knew Two was right-winged.

'Because I cannot open it with my right wing,' replied Two. 'My feet keep taking me to the left and I miss the handle. I was trying to see if I could open it with my left wing instead.'

'What you need is a left-winged door,' replied Far. He was not sure if there was such a thing, but it sounded right.

Two looked at him in surprise. He had not thought of that. 'You are quite right, Far. That was the conclusion I had come to just before you gave me such a fright. Let us go and find Puff.'

They found Puff in the sanctum, playing fish poker with Jack. It looked as if Jack was winning. Puff was glad they had interrupted the game. This gave him an excuse to stop playing. 'Come in, Two. What can I do for you both?'

Two and Far sat down at the table. Two said, 'I need your help, Puff. I want all the doors in the House of Hot Air made left-winged. That way I will not have to bump into them every time I try to open them.'

Puff was a little bewildered. He had never heard of a left-winged door. He could not admit he did not know. He turned to Jack and asked, 'A strange request, don't you think, Jack? What would you say to Two?'

'I would ask Two to show me a left-winged door.' replied Jack. 'Every door has its handle on the left side on one side, and on the right side when you are on the other side of the door. There is no such thing as a left-winged door, so, if you do not mind, we will return to our game. It is your turn, Puff.' Jack knew he was winning and he wanted to beat Puff.

However, Puff was not so easily put off. He had become interested in Two's problem. 'Two is right in a way,' he said quickly. 'If he always uses a door by only going through it one way, then it would always be a left-winged door.

'True,' replied Jack. 'But, having come into a room, how does he get out? Do you intend to make two doors in every room, with one for coming in and one for going out?'

Puff had not thought of that so he could not agree with Jack. 'No,' he replied, 'I have a better idea. I will make all doors into revolving doors. Two will not then have to open them. He will just push them round.' As he said this he flung his arms out, as though he was pushing a revolving door. In doing this, he knocked all the cards on to the floor. 'Oh dear,' he said. 'I have spoilt the game. Never mind, let us go and find a revolving door for Two to try out.'

They found a revolving door at the entrance to the House of Hot Air. 'There you are, Two, try to walk through that and see if it is any easier for you.'

Two shuffled towards the door and, just as he started to push, a penguin pushed from the other side. Two fell into the doorway, was carried round and became stuck in the middle. The door was jammed and would not revolve either way. By then, more penguins had arrived. They were pushing on both sides. Two could not move and was getting very cross in the middle.

Puff decided he had seen enough. He slipped away while everyone was still pushing and shoving to no avail. *That will not work*, he said to himself. *I will have to hope that, by the time Two is extracted from that revolving door, they will have all forgotten about left-winged doors. At least I stopped Jack from beating me at fish poker by knocking all those cards down.* Thinking of this, he chuckled to himself as he quietly returned to his sanctum.

Droll Puff-Puff

Puff did not feel his usual self as he sat on his perch at home. He could not put it down to anything. He had a general feeling that all was not well. Nothing seemed to be going right. They had not yet found much treasure, just a little. In the middle of all this thinking, he fell asleep. He was having a lovely dream. He was riding a white horse in front of his soldiers. He was rudely awoken by someone shaking him and shouting, 'Wake up, Puff! Wake up, please, we need you!' He woke up with a start. It was just as well, as he was about to fall off his horse. He could not ride very well.

It was Doc who had been shouting at him. 'What do you want, Doc? Why must you wake me up so roughly?' grumbled Puff, rubbing the sleep from his eyes. He tried to put his head under his wing and go back to sleep.

Doc was not so easily put off. He shouted again and said, 'You must come at once. Titch wants to make Jack a droll.' The magic word – droll – had the desired effect. Puff was wide awake.

'He cannot do that,' said Puff, struggling to stand up straight. He hopped off his perch and rushed out, followed by Doc. They both went straight to the sanctum. Puff was worried, for he secretly hoped that Titch would make him a droll. Then he could become a wise old bird in a red, feathered cloak. He would not have to worry about all the things which were not working out right.

Puff sat down on his big chair at the head of the table with a flutter of feathers. He saw that Jack was there as well. Turning to him, he said, 'Jack, what is this I hear that Titch is to make you a droll? Is it true?'

Two nearly fell off his chair when he heard this. He did not approve of drolls. He would like to get rid of them all. 'Rubbish,' he shouted. 'Drolls are stupid, old and silly. They should all be abolished. Their upper chamber should be pulled down, so they could not come back.'

'Yes, yes,' said Puff sweetly. 'We all know your views. Let us hear what Jack has to say first.' Turning to Jack, he asked, 'Well, what have you to say?'

'Not very much,' replied Jack. 'I rather like the idea of being a droll. However, it is not true that Titch is going to make me a droll. I do not know what all the fuss is about.'

'You mean he has not asked you to be a droll?' asked Puff in a relieved kind of way.

'No, I did not say that,' replied Jack. 'All I said was, I was not about to be a droll.'

Puff turned to Doc and, thinking about the dream which he had so rudely interrupted, shouted crossly, 'Who told you and why did you wake me up if it is not true?'

Poor Doc stammered and stuttered. He did not know what to say. It seemed as if someone had made a fool of him. The others in the room sniggered to see him so put out, and that did not help him. 'I do not know,' he said at last. 'I do not remember who it was. I was so anxious to tell you, it has slipped my mind.' He sounded very lame but, fortunately for him, Puff was not listening any more. His mind was elsewhere. He dismissed them and sat at the table, brooding.

He was not alone, however, for a voice from the corner said quietly, 'He did offer to make me a droll.' Puff looked up startled and realised Jack was still there. 'But I said no, I do not want—' Suddenly, Jack stopped, and then he said no more. Puff realised there was more to be said from the way he had spoken.

'What do you really want?' asked Puff. 'What did you say to Titch?'

'I told him I want to be head of our penguins,' replied Jack, quietly.

Puff sat back and looked at Jack. 'You mean you want to take over my place as head of our penguins. If you were made a droll, you could not, as drolls cannot be heads. Is that right?'

'Yes,' replied Jack. 'I told Titch I would not agree to being made a droll. I suggested, however, that he made you a droll. Then I could take over as head in your place. Titch thought that was a very good idea. He would give a droll-ship to you as a reward for all your hard and clever work.'

What Titch had not told Jack was the pleasure he would gain from this move. Titch would not have to put up with Puff on the other side of the house. He would rather see Jack there. Puff felt very proud at being rewarded for all his years of work. This gave him a warm glow inside. No one could blame him for becoming a droll for hard work, not even Two. He could leave all his troubles behind. He would not have to worry about finding the rest of the treasure. Jack was much better at worrying than he was. Who knows, he might even find all of the treasure.

Puff cheered up and felt better. Things had turned out for the best at last. He wanted the drollship to be given to him as soon as possible. ' "Arise Droll Puff-Puff" sounds nice to me, sounds nice to me,' he sang as, with a spring in his step, he went on his way to the upper chamber. There, King Peewit the lapwing tapped him on each shoulder with his sword and said, 'Arise, Droll Puff-Puff, and join your peers of the realm in the House of Drolls.'

51

Jack did find the rest of the treasure in time to pay off all the workers. Droll Puff-Puff sat contented, in his red, feathered cloak, in the upper house, with all the other wise old birds. He was now a happy man, and had no more worries.

ARISE DROLL PUFF-PUFF

Printed in the United Kingdom by
Lightning Source UK Ltd., Milton Keynes
137272UK00001B/157-159/P